How to write your letter to Santa

Inside the pocket on the left, you will find
four sheets of writing paper and two envelopes.

Take out the writing paper and
write your name and address at the top.
Then write your Christmas wish list in the spaces.

Next, place your letter in the envelope and copy Santa's address
from the envelope on the left.

You can post your letter up the chimney or in the mailbox
and it will find its way to Santa.

Illustrated by Daniel Howarth
Written by Kath Smith and Becky Brookes

This is a Parragon Publishing book
This edition published in 2006

Parragon Publishing
Queen Street House
4 Queen Street
Bath BA1 1HE, UK

ISBN 1-40545-925-5
Printed in China

Dear Santa...

Written by Kath Smith *and* Becky Brookes

Illustrated by Daniel Howarth

It was Christmas Eve, but Kit was too excited to go to sleep. He didn't know what time it was, but he was sure it was getting very late.

Kit had written Santa a letter, listing all the presents he hoped to get for Christmas.

"I hope I get something from my list," he whispered.

Suddenly, Kit had a terrible thought. He and his family had just moved house, but Kit couldn't remember writing about that in his letter to Santa.

"Oh, no!" groaned Kit, sitting up in bed. "What if Santa still thinks I live at my old house? What if Santa delivers my toys there? What if Santa doesn't visit me here AT ALL ?"

Kit decided to write another letter to Santa. "If I send it up the chimney, it might find its way to him in time," he thought, hopefully.

Kit jumped out of bed and sat at his desk to write a new letter.

Dear Santa,

I'm very sorry but I forgot to tell you I've moved house. I live at 37 Park Road now. Please can you send my presents here instead?

In case you have forgotten, I asked for some new soccer boots, a bike, and a sled.

Lots of love,
Kit
xxxx

P.S. I have tried to be very good this year. Ask my mom and dad.

Kit tucked his letter inside an envelope and addressed it to Santa. Then he tiptoed downstairs, clutching the envelope in his hand.

Kit opened the living room door and was just about to send the note up the chimney, when he heard a loud WHOOSH and a CRASH!

A big black sack appeared in the fireplace, followed by a jolly looking man in a red and white suit.

"Santa, you came!" gasped Kit. Santa stared at Kit in surprise.

"You shouldn't be awake," he chuckled. "But as you're here, you'd better have these."
He pulled out a dolly and a pair of ballet shoes from his sack and gave them to Kit.

"Now don't tell anyone you saw me. Happy Christmas!"

Kit looked at his presents, confused. "B-b-but they're not what I asked for..."

"Aren't they?" asked Santa, looking at his long list of boys and girls.

"I had a letter from this address, written by a little girl called... Aha!"

Santa looked up from the list and peered at Kit. "I see what's happened. You've moved house, haven't you?"

"Yes," replied Kit, handing Santa his envelope. "That's why I wrote you this new letter."

Santa took Kit's note out of the envelope and began to read it.

"Well…Kit," sighed Santa, when he had finished reading, "we had delivered your toys to your old house. But as it was empty, my helpers took them back to my workshop at the North Pole."

"Oh!" said Kit, sadly. "Why did they do that?"

wHOOSH!

"To work out where you live now, of course," Santa chortled. "I don't have time to find every new address AND deliver all the presents, you know!"

With that, Santa clapped his hands three times and the dolly and ballet shoes vanished up the chimney.

Kit felt very badly. He hadn't wanted to cause Santa any trouble. "Sorry," he muttered, glumly. Santa looked at Kit and took the little boy's hand in his big green mitten.

"I'll tell you what," he said, "as I'm running very late, I could do with some help. Would you help me deliver the rest of the presents?"

Kit beamed and nodded his head.

"Yes, please," he said.

This time, when Santa clapped his hands again, both he and Kit flew up the chimney.

"**Wheeeee!**"

cried Kit,
his voice echoing
as he went.

"**Shhh!**" whispered
Santa. "We don't
want to wake
anyone else.

Kit and Santa stood on the roof of Kit's new house.
"Wow! This is the best thing I've ever seen," gasped Kit,
staring open-mouthed at Santa's magical sleigh.
"Hop in, Kit," laughed Santa, "we've got presents to deliver!"
Kit took his seat next to Santa, and with one tug on the reins,
the reindeer flew off into the night, pulling the sleigh with them.

Kit helped Santa unload the presents on each rooftop. Then, Santa slipped down the chimneys of every house, in every street and in every town. At last, all of the sacks were empty.

"Where are we going now?" asked Kit, as Santa's sleigh took off again.

"To the North Pole!" cried Santa, waving Kit's letter. "We're going to find your Christmas presents, Kit."

Kit peered over the edge of Santa's sleigh as it flew higher and higher into the sky. He looked down at all the houses and wondered which one was his new home.

"I can't believe that this is really happening to me," Kit sighed happily to himself.

"Do you like your new house, Kit?" asked Santa.

"It's okay," Kit replied. "We've only just moved so I'm still getting used to everything. I haven't made any friends yet," he added, sadly.

"I'm sure you will soon," Santa winked.

Kit held on tightly, as the sleigh
zoomed through the darkness. The air
became icy cold and Kit's ears began to
tingle.

Suddenly, the sleigh began to swoop
down toward a warm glow in the night.

"Here we are," cried Santa, as the sleigh landed gently in front of a log cabin. "This is my workshop."

The front door to the workshop opened and a sweet little lady appeared.

"Hello, dear," she said. Then, she turned to look at Kit. "Ooh, you must be Kit," she smiled. "I've heard lots about you."

Inside the workshop, Santa led Kit into a room full of busy little elves.

"I've managed to find this little girl's new address," cried one little elf, holding up a piece of paper to Santa. "Shall I put her presents back in your sleigh?"

"They're for the little girl who used to live at your house," Santa whispered to Kit. "This is Kit from 37 Park Road," said Santa to the elf. "Do you know where his presents are?"

"Oh, yes, Santa," replied the elf. "His presents are being loaded into your sleigh. We're just finding the last few missing addresses, then you can deliver all the presents to the right owners."

"Excellent," said Santa. "I'll give Kit a tour of my workshop while we wait."

Kit followed Santa and found himself in another room full of busy elves. This time they were sweeping up wrapping paper...

...and polishing work surfaces. "This is where all the presents are made," said Santa. "But, as you can see, everything's been tidied away now."

Kit was beginning to feel very tired and was trying hard not to yawn.

Suddenly, the door burst open and the little elf from the other room ran in.

"Your sleigh is ready, Santa," he cried. "You had better get going before day breaks."

"Thank you," grinned Santa. "Come on, Kit. Let's take you home, too."

Kit was so tired that he fell fast asleep in Santa's sleigh on the way home.

"Wake up, Kit," Santa soon whispered. "You're home now."

Santa clapped his hands again and Kit found himself magically tucked up in bed.

"Night, Santa," he mumbled before falling asleep again.

The next morning, Kit woke up to find two
wrapped-up presents at the end of his bed.
   "I've got new soccer boots AND a bike!"
he cried. Then, he saw a note addressed to him.

Dear Kit,
Look outside for your final
present. You'll soon discover
it's an extra special one.
Happy Christmas!
Lots of love,
Santa

Kit raced downstairs to open the front door.
He gasped in delight. There, in front of him, was an orange sled.
Kit was just about to sit on his sled, when a boy appeared from next door.

"Wow! What a cool sled!" said the boy. "Did you get it from Santa?" Kit nodded.

"Would you like to ride it with me?" he asked.

"I sure would!" said the little boy. "Did you get everything you asked for this year?"

Kit smiled and nodded.
"And more," he thought to himself.
"I think I've got a new friend too.
Thank you, Santa!"